HENRIETTA
KING
LA PATRONA

MARY DODSON WADE

ILLUSTRATIONS BY
BILL FARNSWORTH

bright sky press
HOUSTON, TEXAS

bright sky press
HOUSTON, TEXAS

2365 Rice Boulevard, Suite 202,
Houston, Texas 77005

Library of Congress Cataloging-in-Publication Data

Wade, Mary Dodson.
Henrietta King, la patrona / by Mary Dodson Wade ;
illustrated by Bill Farnsworth.
p. cm.
ISBN 978-1-933979-63-2
1. King, Henrietta Chamberlain, 1832-1925—Juvenile literature.
2. Ranchers—Texas—Biography—Juvenile literature.
3. Women ranchers—Texas—Biography—Juvenile literature.
4. King Ranch (Tex.)—Juvenile literature.
5. Philanthropists—Texas—Biography—Juvenile literature.
6. Women philanthropists—Texas—Biography—Juvenile literature.
7. Texas—Biography—Juvenile literature.
I. Farnsworth, Bill, ill. II. Title.

F392.K47W34 2012
976.4'47061092--dc23
[B]   2011052721

Illustrations by Bill Farnsworth
Printed in China through Asia Pacific Offset

TABLE OF CONTENTS

CHAPTER 1
Encounter 5

CHAPTER 2
The Road to Brownsville, Texas 7

CHAPTER 3
The Captain's Courtship 11

CHAPTER 4
Honeymoon in the Wild Horse Desert 15

CHAPTER 5
Two Homes 19

CHAPTER 6
Papa's Pets 23

CHAPTER 7
Surprises, Good and Bad 27

CHAPTER 8
The Running W on the Trail 31

CHAPTER 9
Good Times 35

CHAPTER 10
End of an Era 41

CHAPTER 11
Matriarch of the Ranch 45

CHAPTER 12
Family Matters 49

CHAPTER 13
Doing Good 55

TIMELINE 60

SOURCES 61

AUTHOR'S NOTE 64

CHAPTER 1

....

Encounter

Seventeen-year-old Henrietta Chamberlain stood on the deck of the *Whiteville* in the stifling, humid air. Everything here at the tip of Texas was so different from other places she had lived—the landscape, the weather, even this houseboat that was their home. Her father's missionary zeal had brought them to this town, and she was eager to join his efforts, but what a place this was!

Brownsville was less than three years old in 1849. It had grown up around the fort Zachary Taylor established when his troops were at the mouth of the Rio Grande during the war with Mexico. After Major Jacob Brown died there, the fort and the town took his name. Following an epidemic that left only 500 survivors, the town was booming again. Heavy steamboat traffic on the river had turned it into a major port for the southern United States and northern Mexico. There was a post office and market. Numerous stores lined the banks of the Rio Grande. Soon there would be a proper building for her father's church.

The Reverend Hiram Chamberlain had come to establish a Presbyterian church. The only place available for his family was a houseboat. Undeterred, he held prayer meetings on board the *Whiteville* until the church building was ready.

The slight young woman turned at the noise of a steamer approaching. Suddenly a string of profanity burst from the steamer wheelhouse. The tortuous journey down the Rio Grande had not improved the temper of the tall, dark-haired captain. He stepped out and unleashed his fury at the imbecile who had dared dock in his usual place.

Offended by his language, Henrietta informed the captain in icy tones that no gentleman spoke that way.

Such a rebuke from a man would have brought Richard King's fists smashing into the offender's face. Instead, the twenty-five-year-old captain with the razor-quick temper could only stare at the indignant young woman. He clamped his mouth shut, backed his boat away, and docked at another spot, leaving the five-foot-three-inch, ramrod straight figure standing on the deck of the *Whiteville*.

It was not love at first sight. But then again, maybe it was.

CHAPTER 2

The Road to Brownsville, Texas

Henrietta Morse Chamberlain, born July 21, 1832 in Boonville, Missouri, was the daughter of Reverend Hiram and Maria Morse Chamberlain. Her mother died before she was three years old, and Chamberlain's second wife, Sarah Wardlaw, had died childless. His third wife, Anna Adelia Griswold, would give him eight children. They had buried three infants before they reached Texas.

Hiram Chamberlain had a profound influence on Henrietta's life. The ideals and principles he instilled in her were the basis of Henrietta's lifelong code of conduct. Chamberlain, a native of Vermont, graduated from Princeton Seminary and was an ordained Presbyterian minister. He had a special zeal to "preach the gospel to the poor and ignorant of his own land." The family moved many times as he served various churches in Missouri and Tennessee.

When Henrietta was fourteen, he sent her away to school at the Holly Springs Female Institute in northern Mississippi. The headmaster of the Presbyterian

school was fellow seminarian James Weatherby. The school promised "to provide a thorough and complete education, …aiming at …development of intellectual powers,…formation of the deportment of the most correct walks of society, …cultivation of right motives Christian Morals shall be the prominent feature of instruction."

Henrietta and some ninety classmates studied grammar, arithmetic, history, and foreign languages. Music lessons and art instruction were also available. Henrietta wrote poetry and painted flowers on white velvet.

During the two years Henrietta was there, her father wrote frequently. His long letters were "dictated by the purest affection, and the most unfeigned anxiety for your welfare, and improvement, your happiness and usefulness in the world." Besides family happenings, the letters touched on a wide range of subjects from women's rights to temperance, theology, even personal habits. "Sit up straight," he admonished, "and don't allow yourself to sit in a stooping posture. That will make you round shouldered and ruin you." He encouraged her to read the Bible every day. "The very best knowledge in the world is that which is derived from the Bible."

Henrietta dearly loved her little half-brothers Hiram Jr. and Bland. At school she was very homesick to see them. She sent Hiram Jr. a little book. Her father reported that his son "pretended to read it, and was much pleased that you sent it to him. He professes to understand what you say about him, and becomes very animated." At the same time, he cautioned her to get over being homesick. "That will never do…It will injure your health, and your mind….You must determine to get above it….We were not made to be *perfectly* happy here. We must wait till we get to heaven for that." Her stepmother, with a little more sympathy, enclosed an expensive handkerchief as a present.

Henrietta profited from her father's advice. By the time she arrived in Brownsville she was a calm, efficient, educated young woman of great dignity. The rough language of the riverboat captain shocked her, but she put the whole incident out of her mind.

CHAPTER 3

....

The Captain's Courtship

Twenty-five-year-old Richard King was still smarting from the encounter when his partner James Mifflin Kenedy boarded his vessel. Kenedy, a soft-spoken Quaker, was seven years older than King. Friendship between two such radically different persons would not have seemed possible, but both men respected the integrity and hard work of the other. They forged a bond that lasted a lifetime.

Richard King, born in New York City and orphaned at six, ran away from an apprenticeship at age eleven. He stowed away on a ship and began working on river boats. The only formal education he had was the eight months a sympathetic captain sent him to school in Connecticut. Returning to steamboating on southern rivers, he quickly distinguished himself as a river pilot. Never yielding an inch to anyone, he earned a reputation for fighting and drinking. By age nineteen he was a licensed riverboat captain and had caught the attention of Mifflin Kenedy.

During the war with Mexico, Kenedy saw the

potential to haul supplies for the United States army. He asked King to join him. Their company hauled most of the freight on the Rio Grande.

That day, after discussing the latest business, King made a tentative inquiry about the people living on the *Whiteville*. Guessing the reason for the question, Kenedy could not resist a little fun. He solemnly informed his partner that it was the new preacher's family—a wife, two little boys, and an infant. He didn't mention Henrietta.

King persisted, and Kenedy pretended that he had forgotten about her. King knew that wasn't so. He blurted out a request for introduction.

Half in jest because it seemed ridiculous, but serious because it was true, Kenedy explained that his friend would have to go to prayer meeting to get an introduction. As foreign as it was to him, Richard King agreed.

The actual meeting, however, took place a few days later on a Brownsville street. Afterwards, the rough captain endured long prayer meetings just to get to see the lovely young woman.

Reverend Chamberlain was not pleased at the attention being paid to his daughter. He hoped King's absences carrying freight up the river would end the matter, but he was wrong. When King was in town, he persisted in seeing brown-eyed "Etta."

Henrietta kept busy during King's absences. Melinda Rankin, with Reverend Chamberlain's enthusiastic backing, opened the Rio Grande Female Institute to teach Mexican girls. Henrietta taught English to the girls and in turn learned Spanish. But she looked forward to the times when her handsome suitor returned. He shared exciting plans for the future, and she admired the forceful way "Captain" went after the things he wanted.

Finally, after four years, Henrietta's wishes and King's considerate attention to her broke down her father's resistance. On Sunday evening, December 10, 1854, Richard King arrived at the Presbyterian Church on the corner of Elizabeth and Ninth streets in Brownsville. He took a seat on the front row, staring at his bride-to-be in the choir. After the sermon was over, Reverend Chamberlain performed the marriage ceremony for the captain and the lovely dark-haired young woman wearing a peach-colored ruffled silk gown with sleeves of white lace tied with tiny ribbons.

CHAPTER 4

Honeymoon in the Wild Horse Desert

Henrietta's honeymoon was a four day trip in a large enclosed carriage her husband had bought for the wedding. Her trunks, tied on to the carriage, were packed with clothing, linens, and dishes. Bandits raided the territory where they traveled, and armed outriders guarded them night and day. A cook prepared meals by firelight.

Their destination was a newly formed ranch in the Wild Horse Desert one hundred twenty-four miles north of Brownsville. Herds of wild mustangs roaming the grass-filled prairie gave the area its name.

Richard King had seen this area two years earlier while on his way to a fair in Corpus Christi. Visitors to the fair enjoyed theater performances, lectures, livestock shows, and viewed exhibits such as Gail Borden's non-perishable meat biscuit.

While there, King arranged a partnership with Gideon "Legs" Lewis, whose nickname came from the endurance of his long legs during the Mier expedition. Early in1853, the two paid $300 for 15,500 acres of

the Wild Horse Desert known as the Rincón de Santa Gertrudis. This area just north of Santa Gertrudis Creek, about 45 miles southwest of Corpus Christi, was perfect for raising cattle. Six months later they added another 53,000 acres with the purchase of the de la Garza Santa Gertrudis Grant south of the creek.

They stocked the ranch with Mexican longhorns purchased at $6 a head, and King bought good horses because the mustangs were too wild. He paid more for one stallion than the partners had paid for their first land purchase.

On a trip to Mexico about six months before his marriage, King bought all the cattle in the village of Cruillas (crew-EE-yas). Then, realizing that the people no longer had food or anything left to sell, he offered jobs, homes, and regular pay for anyone who came to Texas to work for him. These skilled *vaqueros* were exactly what he needed to manage his livestock.

More than one hundred men, women, and children formed a procession of people, dogs, chickens, donkeys and creaking carts moving along with the cattle. They settled on the ranch, calling themselves "King's People"—*Los Kineños* (Keh-NIN-yos).

Henrietta's new house turned out to be a *jacal*.

This one-room building had walls made from poles stuck in the ground with mud daubed in the cracks. Undeterred by inconveniences, Henrietta served fresh venison roasts, but the pantry was so small that she had to hang her big platters on the wall outside.

She shared her husband's delight in the place and took the greatest pleasure in riding with him over the unfenced prairie. When she tired, they stopped in the shade of a mesquite tree. He spread a blanket for her to rest while he talked of his plans for the ranch. "I doubt if it falls to the lot of any bride to have had so happy a honeymoon."

CHAPTER 5

Two Homes

The isolated ranch offered the only shelter for people traveling by land between Corpus Christi and Brownsville. A ranch house with covered porch and half-story second floor replaced the *jacal*, and Henrietta played gracious hostess to a stream of people.

The cook prepared hearty meals in a separate kitchen, built away from the house for fire safety. The adjacent dining room was connected to the house by an uncovered walkway. No one, invited guest or stranger, left King Ranch hungry.

A stone commissary stood north of the main house. It had a kitchen, dining area, and sleeping quarters for workers not regularly employed at the ranch. A nearby men's dormitory housed travelers. Still farther north were corals, stables, and sheds for the carriage and wagons. Beyond that was a row of *Kineño* houses. Guarding it all was a watchtower above the commissary and two cannon from King's riverboat days.

Henrietta took a personal interest in *Kineño* families. Because she spoke Spanish, she met their needs.

She nursed the sick and taught the children in her kitchen until a schoolhouse was built. The *Kineños'* fierce loyalty to *La Patrona* gave Richard King peace of mind when he was away from the ranch.

The river freight business often called him back to Brownsville. The Kings built a house next door to the one where Mifflin Kenedy and his bride Petra Vela lived. Here as on the ranch, Henrietta entertained guests.

One of the most famous guests was Lieutenant Colonel Robert E. Lee, who was stationed at Camp Cooper in West Texas more than 600 miles distant. Lee was ordered to Brownsville to sit on a court-martial. King had a contract to carry soldiers guarding the border and met Lee on a trip down the Rio Grande.

Lee found court-martial duty tedious. He relieved the boredom with long solitary walks along the river. In letters to his wife in Virginia, he described the animals and flowers he encountered, and he told her about his visit to the King home. "The King cottage was removed from the street by well-kept trees and shrubbery in the yard, among which were several orange trees filled with ripening fruit. Mrs. King's table was loaded with sweet oranges and many other things tempting to the eye."

Much to the disappointment of the junior officers accompanying him, Lee did not accept an invitation for them to eat with the Kings. He did not consider it a proper thing to do on the first visit.

On May 12, 1860, Lee recorded a visit to the ranch as well, when activities of Mexican folk hero/ bandit Juan Cortina brought him to Brownsville again. He recorded in his memorandum book that day "San Gertrudis—Capt. King's ranch—A beautiful place on a knoll in a mesquite plain, new house." Visits from the courtly middle-aged officer delighted Henrietta.

CHAPTER 6

....

Papa's Pets

The house in Brownsville allowed Henrietta to enjoy her father's family. It also was the place where the first three King children were born.

Henrietta Maria arrived on April 17, 1856. Named for her mother, she became Nettie. Although the Kings usually made the trips between the ranch and Brownsville with armed guards, on one occasion when Nettie was quite small, they were alone. They camped for the night, and Henrietta was tending to the baby when a stranger approached and asked if he might join them. King agreed and turned back to the fire he was building. Henrietta looked up to see the man approaching her husband with a knife in his upraised hand. She called out. King, reacting as he would have in his river brawling days, spun and knocked the man down with one blow. The culprit disappeared, and they had no more trouble the rest of the journey.

Nettie was four days shy of her second birthday when blue-eyed Ella Morse made her appearance on April 13, 1858. Richard King now had two little girls

to brag about.

Two and a half years later, on December 15, 1860, Richard King II was born. This was a double joy—a son to keep the King name alive and someone to take over the ranch empire that continued to grow.

Henrietta enjoyed Brownsville but much preferred to be at the ranch. They spent more time there after their son Richard was born. She had a keen interest in everything going on there.

Alice Gertrudis was born there on April 29, 1862. Of all the children, Alice most resembled her mother in looks. She also came to echo her mother's special love for the ranch.

Richard King reveled in his children. When away from the family, he signed his letters, "my love to all of Pets from Papa."

CHAPTER 7

....

Surprises, Good and Bad

As the ranch grew, so did the herds. Roundup time brought the hot, dusty work of branding the longhorns. Henrietta took the children down to the gathering pens located not far from the ranch house. They ate picnic lunches with their father under nearby trees.

King designed the *Ere Fleche* (R Arrow) brand for himself and used it before his marriage, but the first brand he registered belonged to "Mistress Henrietta M. King, wife of Richard King." It was her joined initials. She rode out one day to find HK branded on the cattle.

Three months after registering the HK, King registered the *Ere Fleche,* but the brand proved to be too complicated. He bought and used several other brands, but in 1869 he began using the simple, hard-to-alter Running W. The famous brand, sometimes called "little snake," became not only the ranch cattle brand but the symbol for King Ranch itself.

The ranch had been in operation just a few years when "Legs" Lewis was killed. Lewis left no will and no heirs for his one-half interest in the ranch. Major W. W. Chapman arranged to buy Lewis' share of the Rincón but backed out when he was sent to California. King then tapped James Walworth, a fellow steamboat captain, to buy the Lewis shares in the huge de la Garza section. When he put Henrietta's name on his half of the huge grant, she owned more land than he did.

The 1860s brought the national conflict over slavery to Texas. Union ships blockaded southern ports. This cut off the money generated by cotton sales.

With other outlets closed, cotton planters sent heavily-loaded wagon to Texas for shipment from Brownsville. The steady stream of wagons crossing King pastures made the ranch a Confederate lifeline. The commissary furnished food, supplies, horses and mules for the final trip to the coastal port.

King and Kenedy were paid in gold to deliver the cotton to waiting foreign ships off shore. To avoid seizure of their vessels, they registered the boats in Mexico. Meanwhile, Richard King joined Captain James Richardson's group of Texas militia and was often away on patrol. *Kineños* guarded the ranch, Henrietta, and the children.

In late 1863 twenty-six Union transport ships

anchored at the tip of Texas. The commander at Fort Brown abandoned the fort and burned all the cotton awaiting shipment. Fire gutted many of the buildings in town.

Word came to the ranch that Union soldiers were approaching. Henrietta's fifth child was due in two months. Although her father was with her, Richard King was in Mexico. Believing that the unarmed family was safe, she chose to stay at the ranch.

At dawn two days before Christmas, a troop of more than seventy soldiers rode into the yard yelling and firing guns. Francisco Alvarado, staying in the house for added protection, was shot and killed before he could explain that only the family was present.

Henrietta told the soldiers that her husband was not home. Angry at missing the object of their search, they turned their fury on the house. They urged horses through the door, slashed curtains, broke open trunks, destroyed furniture, and smashed mirrors and dishes. As they left, they took all the horses they could corral.

Realizing it was not safe to remain, Henrietta packed what she could. On Christmas Day the children climbed into the coach with their mother, and Reverend Chamberlain accompanied them to San

Patricio. On February 22, 1864, Henrietta's fifth child was born. She named him Robert E. Lee to honor the commander of the Confederate army.

CHAPTER 8

....

The Running W on the Trail

After the Civil War ended, Union authorities occupying Texas seized all of the King property. Because he was wealthy, King needed a presidential pardon to have it returned.

While they waited, Henrietta's father died. His widow, Anna Adelia Chamberlain, took her daughter and youngest son Edwin back East. When the Kings finally returned to the ranch in 1867, Henrietta's three half-brothers came too. Soon Edwin returned to join them.

During the conflict the longhorns had multiplied. Bandits stole many thousands of cattle from the ranch, but there were still over 60,000 left. By the time the 1870s came, the ranch became part of the most colorful period in American history.

Fresh beef, very costly in eastern cities, was worth only a fraction of that in the area where cattle lived. There was no refrigeration, so the solution lay in walking the cattle to rail lines where they could be shipped to market. The railroads had reached as far as Kansas,

and cowboys gathered thousands of longhorns and drove the herds to rail depots for shipment.

Unlike other trail drives, the ones from King Ranch had only their own cattle. In early 1876, they had 30,000 head of cattle ready to go to Kansas. The sight of a King Ranch drive made a tremendous impression. "The horses were uniform and beautiful. They had long manes and tails….There would be bay horses with red cattle, black horses and black cattle, brown horses with brown cattle."

King used his own employees to move his cattle. He called the ones in charge "Kansas Men," because that was most often their destination. Unlike most trail bosses, they shared in the profits from the sale of the cattle. King did not accompany the herds but met the partners at their destination and settled accounts. One drive in the 1870s netted him $50,000.

The Running W brand became widely known. On a later trail drive to Cheyenne, Wyoming, herd boss Walter Billingsley reached a small town in Nebraska. He needed cash to pay off five cowboys who had been fired for getting drunk and failing to return to the herd. When Billingsley went to the town bank to borrow $600, the banker did not know him and refused to give him money. Billingsley went back to the herd and returned with the 150-horse remuda, along with the chuck wagon. All were blazoned with the Running W. "If that is not enough," he told the banker, "I have fifty-six hundred steers out there about three miles, all the same brand." Billingsley got the money.

CHAPTER 9

....

Good Times

King continued to buy land. With bandits roaming unsettled areas, he traveled with a shotgun and five or six *Kineño* guards. Camps twenty-five miles apart furnished fast horses and strong mules for relays. Often large sums of money lay hidden in a secret metal box inside his coach. Only Henrietta and the ranch accountant knew of its existence.

King bought large and small areas of land to solidify his patchwork of holdings, using lawyers to search Spanish and Mexican land grant records to find owners. He finally amassed over 600,000 acres using the services of his long-time friend, Brownsville lawyer Stephen Powers.

When Powers died, King turned to Powers' bright young partner Jim Wells. The new lawyer, unsure how to proceed, asked how often he should report. "Young man, the only thing I want to hear from you is when I can move my fences."

The ranch house grew along with the ranch. It was remodeled and refurbished. The roof was raised,

adding bedrooms in a full second story for the growing children. A governess and a tutor came to teach them. The increasing number of visitors dictated a larger kitchen and dining room as well.

Henrietta continued to oversee her family and the needs of the *Kineños*. She maintained a strong interest in ranch activities but did not confine herself there. She traveled along on her husband's business trips to San Antonio, Galveston, New Orleans, and St. Louis, Missouri.

Following a trip to Kentucky to buy horses, they went to Virginia so that Lee could meet the famous general whose name he bore. General Lee loved children and complimented his namesake on his new blue suit. Then, turning to Henrietta with a twinkle in his eye, he added that the color was not his favorite. Only then did she realize her mistake in choosing a suit the color of Union army uniforms.

In the early 1870s, Nettie and Ella enrolled in the Henderson Female Institute, a Presbyterian school in Danville, Kentucky. Alice soon joined them briefly, then the two younger girls transferred to Mrs. Cuthbert's Seminary in St. Louis, Missouri.

Richard II entered Centre College, the Presbyterian

school in Kentucky that his uncle Hiram Jr. had attended. Richard King sent along a carriage and servant for his older son. Lee later enrolled in the same school, but his heart was in the ranch—he much preferred to work alongside the *Kineños*. Lee switched to a St. Louis business college to learn how to help run his father's business.

Henrietta visited the girls. Impetuous as always and wealthy enough to buy what he wanted, Richard King showered his children with extravagant gifts. Henrietta tried in vain to curb his choices. On one occasion he wrote his wife, "See that none of Papa's pets wants for anything money will buy."

When Nettie married Major Edwin Atwood in 1878, the St. Louis newspaper was agog at the lavish gifts presented to the bride. Three years later, Ella chose the ranch house for her marriage to Louis Welton. The following year son Richard took Pearl Ashbrook as his bride. The Kings gave them a 40,000-acre ranch, as well as the cattle brand with Henrietta's initials.

Henrietta received her share of gifts, but she was at a loss the day he appeared with a pair of flawless diamond earrings. Her strict upbringing taught that it was sinful to display wealth, but refusing to wear her husband's gift would make her seem ungrateful. She solved the problem by having a jeweler cover them with dark enamel.

CHAPTER 10

End of an Era

Terrible drought covered South Texas in the early 1880s. Stock tanks dried up. King complained, "Where I have grass, I have no water. And where I have water, I have no grass."

Then, in August 1882, thirty-three-year-old Bland Chamberlain died of a fever. Sorrow became unbearable a few months later when the family received a telegram from St. Louis saying that Lee was seriously ill with pneumonia. They rushed to his side. His death on March 1, 1883, was so overwhelming that Henrietta became seriously ill. With her mother unable to return to the ranch, Alice accompanied her father home to act as hostess.

King lost interest in the ranch, and word reached Henrietta that he planned to sell. Buyers came to look over a hastily gathered herd and were overwhelmed when they saw 12,000 animals. King was not pleased. "Why did you gather such a small herd?" He gave orders to have a larger herd the next morning. The astonished buyers, learning that four or five times that number of cattle could be brought in, left and never made an offer.

Spirits began to lift when rain returned in July. "My Dear Wife," he wrote. "We are all well and the grass in the yard is green once more."

About this time, Robert Justus Kleberg joined a Corpus Christi law firm. The young lawyer's skill in representing opponents in a lawsuit brought by King and Kenedy caused the two friends to lose their case. King was so impress with Kleberg that he hired him. Before long, Kleberg was handling most of the ranch legal work.

Kleberg's family was prominent in Texas. His education and law degree were the result of a legacy from his great-great-uncle in Germany. His polished manners impressed Henrietta, and his quick mind and interest in the ranch impressed her husband. Before long, Kleberg and Alice King developed a deep attraction to each other. Both parents considered him a worthy candidate for his daughter's hand. The two young people became engaged in 1884, but the wedding was postponed because of her father's health.

Richard King was seriously ill with stomach cancer, dulling the pain with liquor. Mifflin Kenedy urged his friend to get medical help. Henrietta pushed him to see a doctor in San Antonio. After examining his patient at the Menger Hotel, the doctor told Henrietta that King's drinking was making things worse. Henrietta quietly advised the doctor how to approach the subject of quitting alcohol. "Tell him with a smile that I need him a while longer."

King, hearing the doctor's edict, stormed into his wife's room. "Etta. Did you say you needed me a while longer?" Nothing else was overheard. The drinking stopped, but the disease did not. On April 14, 1885, Mifflin Kenedy, grieving the loss of his beloved Petra Vela, stood with the family at Richard King's bedside as he died.

By the terms of the will, King left everything "to my beloved wife, Henrietta M. King, to be by her used and disposed of precisely the same as I myself might do were I living." For the next forty years, the diminutive widow dressed in black would be the matriarch of the vast empire.

CHAPTER 11

....

Matriarch of the Ranch

Fifty-three-year-old Henrietta King returned to the ranch. A few weeks after the funeral, she copied English poet George Bank's popular inspirational poem and pasted it in her scrapbook.

What I Live For
I live for those who love me
For all human ties that bind me
For the good that I may do.

She was a millionaire, with 614,140 acres of land, 40,000 head of cattle, 6,600 horses, 500 mules, and 12,000 sheep. But she also inherited heavy debts. The day King left the ranch for the last time, he instructed lawyer Wells "not to let a foot of dear old Santa Gertrudis get away from us."

Henrietta sold a few pieces of land, but ten years later, the debts were gone. She continued to buy land, following the advice she said came from Robert E. Lee—"Buy land; and never sell."

She kept a firm hold on the ranch and the household. She placed her husband's picture on ranch letterhead. Several portraits of Richard King hung in the house, and she constantly wore a brooch with his likeness.

Robert J. Kleberg and Alice, waiting a respectful time after her father's death, married in a quiet affair at the ranch July 17, 1886. Kleberg now sat at the other end of the long dining table, while Alice sat next to her mother.

Henrietta was sole proprietor of the ranch, and Kleberg made no decisions without consulting her. At the outset, he knew little of day-to-day ranching operations and leaned heavily on the advice of the trusted stockmen who had worked for King. He learned Spanish so he could talk with the *vaqueros*. After nearly ten years of observing Kleberg's diligent work, Henrietta gave him Power of Attorney to act in all legal and financial matters concerning her property.

She rarely interfered with decisions. On one occasion, though, an elderly *Kineño* was fired after refusing to give up his whip. When he came to say goodbye to *La Patrona,* Henrietta investigated the circumstances. The matter was resolved with the *Kineño* staying, but whip was gone.

Twice a year Henrietta rode in the big coach to visit each cow camp. She knew the workers, the cattle, and the land.

Cattle sales were a main source of ranch income. Richard King had improved the herds by cross-breeding longhorns with other breeds. When Kleberg introduced shorthorns into the herd, they carried even more weight. He had fences built to kept herds separated so that orders could be filled as needed.

The horse and mule operation produced fine carriage horses as well as mounts for the army and metropolitan police departments. Fifteen years after Richard King died, the ranch was one of the world's largest commercial producer of horses and mules.

Kleberg built the first cattle dipping vat for Tick Fever. Cattle plunged into the long chute and swam out the other end. Medication in the water killed the ticks that carried Tick Fever.

Another severe drought in the 1890s sent thousands of starving Mexicans to the ranch. They were hired to clear pastures by chopping mesquite with axes, picks and grubbing hoes. Each worker received food and wages. Although some left after getting food, nobody went after them. Henrietta King issued a standing order that no hungry person was ever to be turned away from her ranch without food and the offer of a job.

Water was so scarce that cattle ate prickly pear cactus after *vaqueros* singed off the thorns. The situation became so desperate that Henrietta paid $1000 to send explosives aloft in balloons. The noise from detonation was supposed to cause rain, but the rain-making experiment was a failure.

Kleberg advised Henrietta to bring in heavy machinery to dig for water. "This will cost money but we need it to make land worth anything." He instructed the crew to keep on boring until their drill bit "came out on the other side of the earth unless they found water sooner." In June 1899, they struck water. Windmills soon dotted pastures.

CHAPTER 12

....

Family Matters

Henrietta traveled to other cities to see her grandchildren. At the ranch, the Klebergs gave her five more grandchildren between 1887 and 1898. The first Kleberg boy was named Richard Mifflin for the two river captains. Then came Henrietta Rosa, carrying the name of both of her grandmothers. The next granddaughter had her mother's name, Alice Gertrudis. The fourth child was Robert Justus Kleberg, Jr. The youngest daughter, Sarah Josephine, was named for Mifflin Kenedy's daughter, the wife of Dr. Arthur E. Spohn.

The frame house was enlarged a third time, with ten new rooms to accommodate children, ranch managers, and guests. Galleries around the house provided a place for the children to roller skate. They were a normal, active lot. Each had assigned chores, but they all enjoyed horseback riding. They knew ranch work and had *Kineños* for playmates.

Henrietta often took her sewing and church newspaper out on the first floor gallery. Here, she discussed ranch business with her son-in-law. The children often

gathered around for her stories. Any misbehaving child might feel the rap on the ankle from her cane.

Dinner was a formal affair announced by three bells. The first bell called everyone to wash up. Women donned fresh dresses, and men put on suit coats. Offenders, even guests, were sent to change. At the second bell, everyone gathered in the parlor. When the third bell sounded, Henrietta led the way to the dining room. In times of rare rain, Henrietta held a newspaper over her head along the uncovered walkway.

After dinner, everyone gathered in the music room. Robert Kleberg sang old favorites. The children chimed in with songs the *Kineños* had taught them. The last song was always a hymn, especially Henrietta's favorite, "Rock of Ages."

There was a strict rule against dancing, card playing, and alcoholic beverages. The children hid their cards for a new game called Flinch. Bouncy little Henrietta, deemed "butterfly" by her grandmother, begged, "Can't I *dance* instead of playing hymns?" She knew the answer, but Alice Kleberg sometimes quietly offered the young people an alternative, "Let's have a dance on the prairie!"

The rule against dancing relaxed once a year. At

Christmas time the family celebrated with the *Kineños* at their holiday dance. *La Patrona* presented presents to everyone—clothes, petticoats, and jackets for the grownups and a bright red stocking overflowing with candy and fruit for the children. Part of the Christmas preparations at the big house each year was the making and filling of the stockings.

When the Kleberg children were old enough to go to school, Henrietta built an oranate Victorian house in Corpus Christi for use on school days. Henrietta was not active in the town's social set but enjoyed entertaining friends and family. She did, however, entertain President William Howard Taft when he came to Corpus Christi, giving him a Running W saddle. Her main joy in town came from attending the First Presbyterian Church. She provided money for a new church building in her husband's memory.

Staying in Corpus Christi also allowed her to be near Dr. Spohn, her personal physician. He had saved her brother Willie's life after Willie was bitten by a rabid coyote. Dr. Spohn had also delivered all the Kleberg children. Alice raised money to build a modern hospital named for the doctor. Her mother made a generous gift of land and money.

Henrietta continued to travel, taking family trips to places like Colorado Springs, Colorado. Thirteen trunks went with her.

CHAPTER 13

Doing Good

Henrietta endorsed her son-in-law's idea for a rail line between Corpus Christi and Brownsville. She made the largest donation of land for the right of way, and on July 4, 1904, she was on hand to meet the first train that arrived. Standing up in her carriage, she exclaimed, "Thank goodness it is here!"

The company repaid Henrietta by issuing her the first annual pass. Alice Kleberg and her children got the second one. The train did not run on Sunday in respect for Henrietta's feelings about working on that day.

The place where Henrietta greeted the train was three miles from the big ranch house. It became the town of Kingsville. She was major stockholder in the Kleberg Town & Improvement formed to develop a town. The company laid out streets and named many of them for family members. Lot sales were tightly controlled so the town grew in an orderly fashion. Because of Henrietta, no liquor could be sold in the town. Within a year, one thousand people had moved there.

The town's first permanent business, The Kingsville

Lumber Company, belonged to her. She also owned the newspaper published by the Kingsville Publishing Company. The Kingsville Power Company, built mostly with her funds, brought electricity to the town in 1908. She financed the first cotton gin in the area and eventually owned most of the cotton gins between Corpus Christi and Brownsville.

She gave money for churches and schools. The first church service in Kingsville was held in the unfinished building at her lumberyard. She donated both site and money to construct the Presbyterian Church. Soon the Baptist, Methodist, Episcopalian, Catholic, and Christian churches received land for their buildings. She provided funds for a two-story brick school building with twenty-two rooms. She gave the Presbyterian Synod of Texas land to build a vocational training school for Mexican boys.

She was at the ranch when the house caught fire on January 4, 1912. Grandson Richard's bulldog, barking and pulling on covers, woke his master. Everyone got out safely, but some guests sleeping on the second floor were injured when they jumped after fire blocked the stairs.

Eighty-year-old Henrietta put on her black dress

and came outside carrying two small bags. One had her medicine, the other some valuables. When men started to go back to remove furniture, she stopped them. "We can build a new home. We can't replace a life." As heat forced the bystanders to move away, Henrietta turned and threw a kiss to the house that held so many memories.

Kleberg started immediately on plans for a new home. Henrietta had only one instruction. "Build a house that anybody could walk in *in boots.*" Kleberg wanted the great house to be a monument to his mother-in-law's hospitality and fashioned it after a residence he had seen in Mexico.

When finished in 1915, the gleaming white stucco house had twenty-five rooms, each with a fireplace, and almost as many bathrooms. The dining hall seated thirty-two people. Tropical trees and flowers graced the enclosed patio. Tiffany glass filled the tower windows. Tile covered all the floors except the salon, where the floor was made of teak and rosewood inlay. Henrietta would live here for the last ten years of her life.

Those years found raiders from Mexico again attacking ranch property. A searchlight was placed on the tower, and men with loaded rifles braced for an attack on the house. Henrietta insisted on seeing the preparations. Satisfied, she said, "I'm going to bed. Every thing seems in order." No raids reached the big house.

About the time of World War I, ranch income plummeted. Henrietta loaned money. The huge ranch got even larger when several debtors settled their notes by signing over land to her. She bought other ranches and added odd sections of land to make her holdings in solid groups. Eventually, there were four separate divisions.

Grateful for all that Alice had done, Henrietta deeded the Santa Gertrudis headquarters and house to her. To her son-in-law, she gave 3/32 interest in the rights to any minerals found anywhere on her land.

By the time of her death on March 31, 1925, Henrietta King had outlived all of her children except Alice. Her body lay in a bronze casket in her great house as friends, family, and employees came to say goodbye. After a simple funeral, a mile-long cortege wound out of the ranch to the cemetery in Kingsville. Nearly two hundred *vaqueros*, some of whom had ridden for two days, accompanied the hearse on horses branded with the Running W.

At the grave site, *Kineños* stood next to dignitaries.

As the casket was being lowered, the riders mounted and cantered single file around the grave, hats lowered toward *La Patrona.*

After they rode away, the mound of fresh earth lay covered with flowers. Among them was a handmade bouquet of yellow huisache and a Running W made of wildflowers.

TIMELINE

1832 .... July 21, born in Boonville, Missouri,
to Maria Morse and Hiram Chamberlain

1835 .... mother dies, father remarries

1847-49 ... attends Female Institute of Holly Springs,
Mississippi

1850 .... in Brownsville, Texas, with father, his third wife,
and little brothers

1854 .... teaches briefly at Rio Grande Female Institute
in Brownsville

1854 .... December 10, marries Richard King

1856 .... Henrietta Maria (Nettie) born

1858 .... Ella Morse born

1860 .... Richard II born

1862 .... Alice Gertrudis born

1863 .... ranch house overrun by Union soldiers
on horseback

1864 .... Lee born, named for General Robert E. Lee

1869 .... Running W registered as official brand,
still used today

1885 .... April 14, Richard King dies. Henrietta inherits
approximately 500,000 acres of land and about
$500,000 of debt

1886 .... July 17, Alice marries Robert Justus Kleberg

1904 .... town of Kingsville established

1912 .... original ranch house burns

1915 .... completion of large new house

1925 .... March 31, dies at ranch and is buried
in Kingsville

SOURCES

"preach the gospel..." Rev. Hiram Chamberlain, Scrapbook 1. Kingsville, Texas, King Ranch Archives.

"to provide a thorough..."*Holly Springs Gazette*, 30 December 1841.

"dictated by the purest..." Hiram Chamberlain to Henrietta Chamberlain, October 16, 1846. Archives.

"Sit up straight..." and "The very best knowledge..." Hiram Chamberlain to Henrietta Chamberlain, December 2, 1846. Archives.

"pretended to read it..." and "That will never do..." Hiram Chamberlain to Henrietta Chamberlain, January 22, 1847. Archives.

"I doubt if ..." Henrietta King, note, King Ranch vault, in Tom Lea, *The King Ranch* (Boston: Little, Brown and Company, 1957), 128-129.

"The King cottage..." Robert E. Lee to Mary Custis Lee, December 1856. Lea, 143.

"San Gertrudis..." R.E. Lee, Memorandum Book No. 3, May 12, 1860. Library of Congress, Washington, D.C., quoted in Lea, 167.

"my love to all..." Richard King, letters, Archives.

"Mistress Henrietta…" Nueces County (Texas) Registry of Brands. Lea, 402.

"The horses were uniform…" John Maltsberger, Lea, note, 462.

"If that is not enough…" A.W. Billingsley, Lea, 363

"Young man…" Robert C. Wells, Lea, 339.

"See that none of Papa's pets…" R. King, Lea, 343-44.

"Where I have grass…" R. King, Lea, 351.

"Why did you gather…" Ramón Alvarado, Lea, 357.

"My Dear Wife…" R. King, July 8, 1883, King Ranch vault. Lea, 358.

"Tell him with a smile…" and "Etta, did you say…" Alice and Robert J. Kleberg, Sr, to Richard M. Kleberg, Sr. Lea, 368.

"to my beloved wife…" R. King, will, filed April 23, 1885, recorded *Probate Minutes*, Nueces County, (Texas), Vol. F., pp.16-17.

"not to let a foot…" R. King to James Wells. Lea, 366.

"Buy land…" Henrietta King, family reminiscence. Lea,145.

"This will cost…" and "come out on…" R.J. Kleberg to H. King, memorandum. Lea, 504.

"Can't I *dance*…" Henrietta Rosa King. Lea, 561.

"Let's have a dance…" Alice G.K. Kleberg. Lea, 521,

"Thank goodness…" H. King. Lea, 544.

"We can build…" H. King. Lea, 570.

"Build a house…" H. King. Lea, 571.

"I'm going to bed…" H. King. Lea, 590.

AUTHOR'S NOTE

In 1982, Henrietta King was elected to the National Cowgirl Hall of Fame in Fort Worth, Texas.

Henrietta King's will stipulated that the ranch could not be broken up until ten years after her death, allowing the ranch to continue operation while partitioning among heirs took place. Today, the vast ranch, the largest in the mainland United States, consists of four divisions: Santa Gertrudis, Laureles, Encino, and Norias. Although still family owned, it is run as a corporation with headquarters in Houston, Texas.

Neither Henrietta nor Robert Kleberg lived to see oil and gas production on the ranch, but the Kleberg children profited from the mineral rights their grandmother gave to their father.

Hunting is allowed on some parts of the ranch, but other areas are off limits. After wildlife became scarce, Caesar Kleberg, nephew of Robert J. Kleberg, Sr., worked to establish state game preserves. King Ranch now serves as a model for restoring wildlife to a habitat.

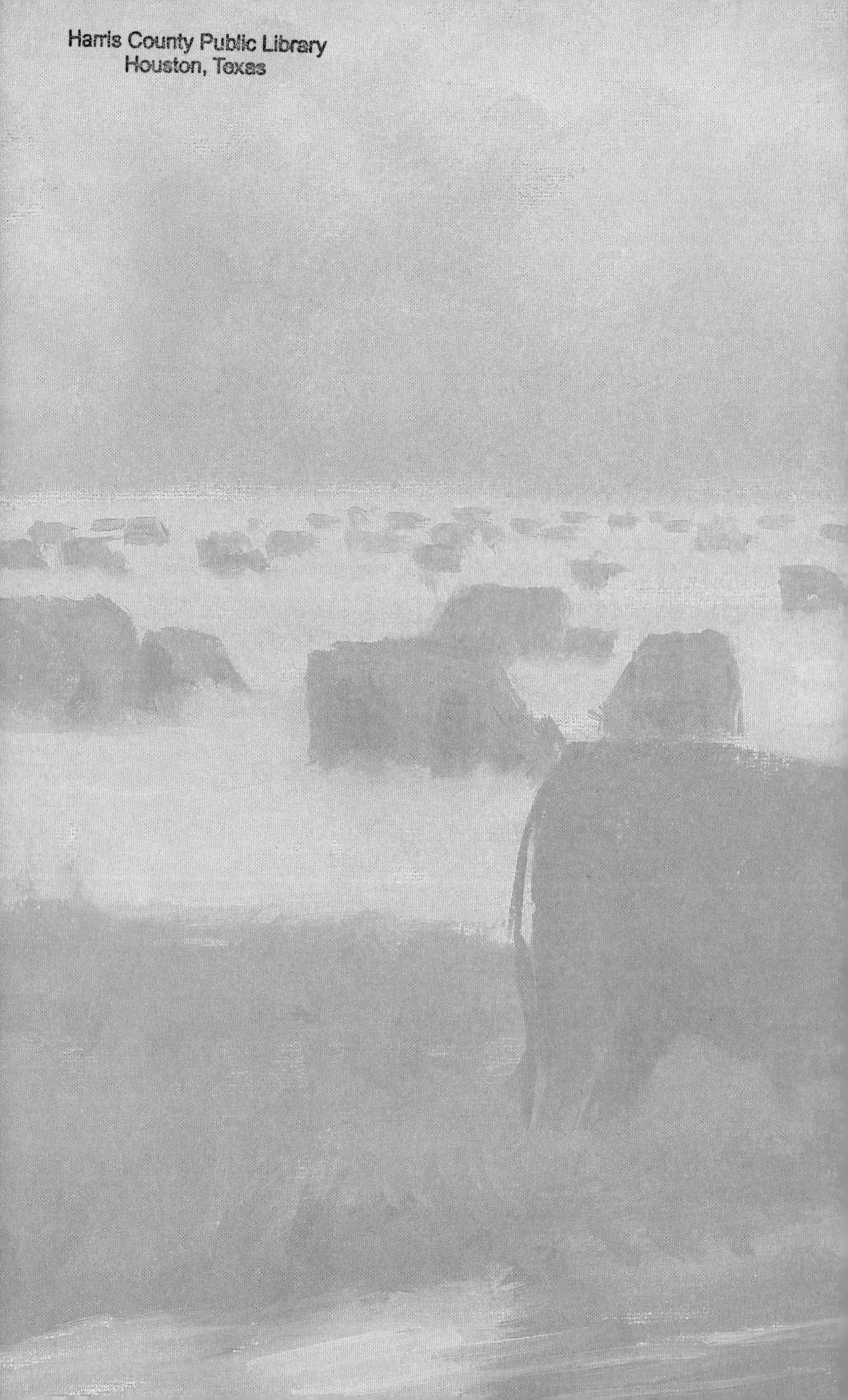